SEPHARDIC LOLITA

SEPHARDIC LOLITA

Judeo-Arabic Restoration and Reconciliation

Dr. David Rabeeya

Library of Congress Control Number:		2006904321
ISBN:	Hardcover	1-4257-1732-2
	Softcover	1-4257-1656-3

This is a work of fiction. Names, characters, places and incidents either are the product of the author's imagination or are used fictitiously, and any resemblance to any actual persons, living or dead, events, or locales is entirely coincidental.

To order additional copies of this book, contact:
Xlibris Corporation
1-888-795-4274
www.Xlibris.com
Orders@Xlibris.com

34536

CONTENTS

SEPHARDIC LOLITA

RECAPTURING MY IRAQI PAST: JUDEO-ARABIC MYTHOLOGY RESTORED

FAREWELL, MY PRECIOUS PAST: JEWISH IRAQI EPILOGUE

Dedicated to my beloved Arlene,
who is my Muse and my inspiration

SEPHARDIC LOLITA

DR. DAVID RABEEYA

CHAPTER I

Habiba the Girlish One

It all began in the streets of Marrakesh in the Jewish sector many, many generations ago. She had the beauty of a Berber Arab and Jewish in her blood. She was born small, but with incredible feminine assets. Her large braziers could not contain her flourishing bosoms. Her hair was long, black, and silky. Above her penetrating and almond-like eyes one could detect the bluish decorative lines. She always wore a Star of David, which often was buried in the dept of her warm and smooth, brown chest.

Only on Jewish holidays would she wear her white blouses and white skirts. White was supposed to represent a life of purity and virginity in the dark streets of the Moroccan scene. She was thirteen, her period had already occurred several times. Her mother taught her all that she needs to know about this life's bloody cycle. Rags were placed after the blood on her private part, and she was told that she is a woman now. She continued to like games with her girlfriends in school. Her idea about being a woman was a combination of a sharp smell, flowing liquids, fear and anxiety. Her head was always covered when she was outside her house. She automatically collected her shining attractive hair into her head cover. In her place she was told that a woman's hair was the finest attraction when a man sees the female genders of the world.

Moroccan Arab-Jews were saturating in the cultural juice of the Arab-Muslims and Berbers. She was not allowed to sit on her father's lap from the age of seven lest she will arouse him sexually. Taboo over taboo. Her family took everything from their environment, but somehow their Jewishness shows in her face morning and evening. She had an Arabic name. A name like Habiba can easily cover your Jewish persona, but it makes sense also in

Hebrew. Like her name, she was loved by her father, the cantor of the brick and straw synagogue on the top of the Atlas Mountains. She was also loved by her teenage relative young man, who could not stop sinning in his heart at her sexual appearance. She was oozing with it. Her mother was convinced that Habiba is ready for a Jewish wedding.

"Marry them young," she always volunteered to say. "In this way they will fulfill the commandments of 'be fruitful and multiply,' and they can have sex to have some relaxation. There is no harm in catching two birds with one stone."

Habiba was busy doing the chores in her one room house. The two mules of her family were tied to a rusty pole ready to climb up the steep mountain in order to bring supplies from the convenience store down in the green valley. There were ample caves in the peaks of the Atlas Mountain. People, sheep, and dogs lived in semi-harmony in them, protected from the bitter cold of these cruel lands and soils. Chickens were slaughtered in a kosher fashion in one of the caves. Feathers, blood, and ash were everywhere. Habiba was shocked once when one chicken continued to sway right and left after it was killed. Surrealism was the agenda of this scene. She decided not to eat meat after this horror.

Her veil was dark blue and her abaya was able to cover her, twisting behind her as she walked. Often she asked her mother if she could ride on the mule. Somehow when her body caves have rubbed against the monotonous movement of the mule, it aroused her and offered her an intensive excitement for a while. She did not wish to be killed. In the Atlas Mountains, Berbers and Arab males will sometimes kill their mothers and sisters if they suspect any adulterous activities or loss of virginity before the first sexual encounter with her husband.

Habiba was a fine Jew. She was a religious person, like most Jewish Moroccans. She sat with her mother in a separate section of the shabby looking synagogue, which consisted of a roof made of bamboo and straw. Some bricks were somehow attached to its shabby walls. She prayed hard to Allah-Elohim to send her a decent husband, because her mother told her to do so. She is now an expert in domestic work. Her mother, like a tough sergeant, offered clear instructions on how to pluck the chickens, clean the fish and the meat, dust the room, and mop the floor. She lived with five people in one room: herself, two brothers, and a baby girl. She knows how to change diapers and wash the baby in an old container. Her underwear was larger than she needed in the poverty stricken mountains. The old elastic thread could not often keep it from falling. She needed gently to bring it back to her semi-divine thighs.

She had a way to do it. In her left hand she delicately pushed the elastic to her behind, sometimes touching her semi-bushy vagina. Her expectation from male kisses caused an aroma.

It is hard to believe that she is already thirteen and a half. She knows how to read the holy tongue of Hebrew from the religious prayer books of the Jews. Her mother taught her all she needs to know about the Jewish holidays and customs. She was a believer in her personal God like most Moroccan Jews. She feared Him and prayed to Him with an unusual devotion. Obviously, she spoke to Him in Arabic. After all, this personal God knew Hebrew and Arabic, right? She moved her body with other veiled Jewish women in the women's sections of the synagogue. The more she shook her tender body, the more excited she became about this sensuous procedure. If God is masculine, maybe He can make a move, she thought, in her inner heart. She was trembling with a sudden cold fever, fearing that someone will read her inner, sinful thoughts. Who is this Allah? Does He know about her parents gluing themselves to each other in the freezing nights of Atlas? What does a woman feel when she is penetrated by the fleshy meat of the male? She had already seen blood coming from her body on a monthly basis and she tried to kiss her own nipples. She possessed sensual breasts like ripened pomegranates, brownish and reddish with smooth skin and a greenish-bluish dot on the left. This was her birth mark.

Her family, like many families in these remote mountains, was one of proud Jews living in a remote dream about messianic redemption, in which miraculously they will fly to the Promised Land and build the Holy Temple again. They were both naïve and happy. Mythology was reality in those days. It kept their sanity and gave answers to unanswered questions. Habiba talked a lot with her mother about these forbidden topics. Her father was only present there. She served him his tea with mint leaves, his coffee with cardamom. And his water with lemon and sugar. He also wore his kippa, which looks like the head cover of an Imam. He always made a blessing after eating and drinking. He even washed his hands before he entered the synagogue and the second time after leaving the holy place.

Jewish rituals kept their sanity and gave them some assistance in their minority status among some Muslims, who did not like Jews and tried to convert them to Islam. One day Saleem, the young shepherd, began to brag about his prophet Muhammad. Moses, he said, was a loser. He worked hard and he did not enter the Promised Land. Jesus was also a loser because he was crucified. Only Muhammad died as a victorious man with dignity and pride. Habiba ignored these remarks. She never stopped loving her Judaism despite what others say about it. She loved to meet Saleem when he talked nonsense with his beautiful smile. She loved patting his skinny goats and playing with his dog, Shaytan. There were only about 700 people in her town, and about 200 Jews, who claim to trace their history from the time of the Babylonian Exile in 586 B.C.E. They could not prove it, but the idea was well anchored in their collective mind. They had this perspective that they are only one ring in a long chain of many Jewish exiles ready to climb on the messianic ladder to heaven, like Jacob the Patriarch.

CHAPTER II

Habiba, the Domestic One

By now, Habiba knew how to sew and how to take care of her infant sister. She was almost like a mother: domestic and soft. She was almost ready for the husband to be. Her family Bakovsa had already negotiated with the family of the groom, who goes by the name of Fathi. He was about seventeen with traces of moustache and beard, wearing the Arab long dress, old sandals, and a shiny fez on his head. His name was Jameel in Arabic and Yona in Hebrew. He often masturbated when Habiba was changing her clothes at night. He liked to sneak silently at night with his friends to peak through the walls of her house. He never knew a woman before, and the idea of sleeping with Habiba for a long time was like thinking about real paradise on earth. Jameel had a one track mind, like all men: sexual enjoyment based on touching the soft flesh of the female and evacuating the liquid from their own tense bodies. Jameel, like many men, talked about love, but they mean one specific bodily function. Habiba knew that despite the customs of her society, she needed to learn how to control her curves. After all, she witnessed her mother, Saltana, playing this game with her father, who wished to glue himself to her while his desires were out of control. This was the primitive way of the Moroccan Atlas Mountains, but at the same time, it was real.

The Arabic language in these days did not recognize the concept of privacy. The family was standing outside their home, waiting for Jameel and Habiba to do what millions of men and women do when they are alone. She is expected to pour her blood of virginity on the street and he needed to prove the power of penetration in the pink-reddish-brown flesh. This was not expected by Habiba, kissing, caressing, and fondling skipped by Jameel. He just rushed to evacuate his white, thick fluid in her tube. His parents asked him to fulfill the commandment of Genesis by bringing them a grandson to the world (a granddaughter is accepted with resentment). Habiba, he was told, is the soil, and he is the farmer, who needs to scatter his seeds in to the ground.

To the wedding they invited Berber and Arab neighbors. There was ululation, throwing candies, placing the henna on fingers and toes. This all took place in a spontaneous and emotional fashion. The groom was washed and soaped by his male friends in the spring of the nearby valley. In the synagogue, Jameel read from the Torah, kissed his parents on their hands as a sign of respect, and moved on. Habiba was told that her parents had given Jameel's family two hundred demars. She brought with her two pillows, an old, huge mattress, two heavy blankets, and one wide red sheet with red spring flowers drawn on its center. She also brought candles sticks and matches for the Sabbath ceremony. Jameel promised her in the wedding contract two hundred zoozeem and the matter was settled. She is married. Jameel can know her as much as he wants, whenever he wishes and she must submit. He may praise her bosom and lips when he is lying down upon her, but words of love were not in existence. She was submitting to him with her mouth, behind, and front. The game was control. Jameel demands and Habiba submitted. These were the days, my friend sang. Habiba needed excitement, orgasm, sexual games, and sweet whispers. Jameel was too involved with his organ to think about Habiba's pleasure. He was the jealous type, like residents of his village. Revenging, avenging, settling scores were common themes in this Arab-Berber location. You can rent an Arab, but you cannot own him was one dominant social value in those days. Jameel will kill for the dignity and honor of his wife, but it is also for him to treat her the way he wishes.

Habiba remembered well the scenery of the watch dogs of the local shepherd. The male dog was riding on the back of a bitch. In her mind she identifies with the passive face of the bitch when the male dog is performing his duty. She is like a bitch: passive, submissive, and surrendered to Jameel's wild imagination and fantasies. As it was expected, her mother has told her that a woman should know how to handle her man.

"A woman should know how to trick her man into fine behavior," she proclaimed more than Habiba cared to hear. It is always the woman. Habiba needed Jameel's seeds for her pregnancy and his meager income as an assistant teacher in the elementary religious school. She did not work. She was busy cleaning the house of her mother and father-in-law. She lived with them in one of the rooms with her husband. This was one item in the customs and the mores of the traditional days, may they rest in peace. She frequently looked pale and depressed. Even the powder of her strong rouge and lipstick could not cover the anxiety and the fear in her brown, young face. However, she always smiled to the outside world based on her mother's advice. She revealed beautiful white teeth like Solomon's' lover, Shulamith.

Her mother always invoked Allah's name, who seems to care about everything between married couples except mental and physical abuse. Oh, well!!! Without condoms or any other preventative measures, her stomach began to show signs of swelling. Her baby was cooking slowly in her kitchen womb. Jameel's friends came frequently to the house and she served them Turkish coffee and varieties of nuts. They were gluttonous and rude. They laughed, cursed, sipped out loud, and hugged Jameel after he told them the latest joke about his sexual endeavors.

Like a fly in a spider web, she could only watch the strings develop in a trap without exits and entrances. However, sometimes she looked so cute, so sexy, so delicious, so feminine and delicate. Pregnancy made her so vulnerable, like a light feather floating in the breeze of dawn. Men paid attention to her even more now, especially when she breathed the air in such a feminine fashion. Despite her very large stomach, she managed to maneuver her body in various directions to satisfy her husband at nights. Her father in the next room was moaning and groaning in the excitement of knowing Jameel's mother. Allah, in those days, was present at the time of sex, because men invoked His name during the business of body gluing.

She gave birth to a beautiful girl by the name of Samira. Her husband and his family were behaving like persons in mourning. Why? They asked Allah for a boy, and Allah delivered a girl.

"Who is going to read the Kaddish when he dies of old age?" they asked. "Who can find money for her dowry? Who can find a husband with means in order to sustain her when she is to be married? Who will plow the small land around the shack? Who will show the muscles of the body for the world to see? None!"

Suddenly, far away from the Jewish Moroccan group, aggressive and idealistic European Jews were successfully building a Jewish state. It was a brutal and bloody way. These Zionist Jews entered into the heart of the Arab culture and asked to be recognized as permanent citizens of the Middle East. They won and, therefore, they considered themselves right in their ideology. Some of them also adopted Carl Marx and Ben Katzemelson as fathers instead of her Allah. While Palestine was on fire and misery has been created to handle hundreds of thousands of souls, she was nursing Samira. Her bosom had expanded and to them were added blue veins.

CHAPTER III

Habiba, the Business Woman

Somehow rumors about moving to European Israel were in the air followed by human earthquakes. Masses of Moroccan Jews left their history and mythology and began flying to the land which the God of Genesis promised in His Biblical texts to give to his descendents. The only difference was that most European Jews did not wait for God to deliver on His promises. They took arms against the Arabs and won. After all, God had always followed the victors.

In the transitional camp of the European Israel, Habiba faced poverty, oppression, and negligence. Suffice it to say, the European Israel was not designed for an Arab-Jewess like her. In the city of tents, many men from many ethnic and cultural backgrounds could not ignore their basic biological needs and she was ready to make some income. These shallow routine moments of these encounters had changed this beautiful, religious Jewish princess into an independent, aggressive Israeli woman, who had control over her marketing body. One moment Habiba was submissive to the hand of Allah, her husband, and her Jewish-Arab heritage, and then the next moment she became a container collecting the male seeds of strangers. Her income was impressive and her name was spreading among married men and bachelors in the filthy tent city. Many whores were walking between the pitched tents of the tent city of her settlement. Arab-Jewish men stood unshaved and bitter. These were the days of redemption for many European Jews who built the Jewish state.

Habiba left Samira in the leaking tent with her mother. Innocently, she escorted a man who looks for the tent of fartuna, the lady of the night. Poverty joined cultural shakes to convince him to try it for a fine fee. She charged ten shekels if the man wanted her to lie down on her back, and only five shekels if she bends her head to the ground in order for the client to reach her from her toasty behind.

This quick metamorphosis has occurred without even her knowledge, as if someone kidnapped her Judeo-Arabic traditions. Habiba's mother babysat for Samira and Habiba babysat lonely, horny Ashkenazic men from the nearby village and desperate Sephardic men from the tents. Her husband was only staring at the horizon, spitting into space. He was cursing the European Jewish state in the Berber, Arabic and the French languages. He could not control his Habiba anymore. She did not pay attention to Allah, to him, nor to his father. Her body suddenly became exclusively her body, a machine ready and able to absorb the seeds in the many condoms to live the life of freedom according to her mind. All Jewish prayers of Morocco about redemption and Holy Land sounded like fast flashes of lightening. They come and go in an instance. The prayers about Allah-Elohim and His miracles looked like bad jokes, she thought. Here, in Israel money talks and money brings status, and status brings good life. Believing in Allah and living a humble existence under God's open eyes seemed to her now as a nightmarish legend told by charlatans who wished to control Moroccan Jews in their caves of the Atlas Mountains.

Well! Her clients kept coming. Her father continued to pray his innocent prayers, unable to speak Ashkenazic Hebrew. Her mother knew about Habiba's profession in the land of the Ashkenazic planet, but she was unable to do much about it. Habiba brought shekels and ate well with her husband in the middle of the austerity which existed in the fifties. Her face continues to shine with feminine desire and her body continued to project the desire for the bodies of men. After awhile, she began to notice the bad breath of many of her clients and their demands for unusual and bizarre activities for their payments. Like her daughter, Samira, she consented to the practice of sucking the masculine limb for extra shekels. For another shekel or two she accepted a pack of expensive American cigarettes in return for heavy slapping on her guitar-like, young behind. And then came the Iraqi Jew, full of himself, dressed up like the rich Arabs in Iraq. He was all faranzi in his meticulous, expensive clothes. On his index finger sat a huge golden ring with an incredible precious stone on top. His necklace was shinning over his hairy chest. An impressive watch from Switzerland and French leather red shoes only added importance to his walk. He was a very generous and very demanding client.

She submitted to him because he behaved like a gentleman, always whispering his unusual sexual favors. His voice was soft and almost delicate.

Only the Iraqi client was allowed to remain on her after he spread his heavy liquids directly in her warm, desirable womb. Only the Iraqi was allowed to have her private part as a meal of a hungry man in heat. He came to Palestine ten years before the establishment of the European Israel. His father, he told Habiba, was a rabbi in a well-known, prestigious synagogue. His mother and his many brothers and sisters migrated to Australia. They were the smart types. They heard about the trouble in the Jewish state, and they did not wish for their sons and daughters to die with their Palestinian counterparts as sacrifices to the Molech of war. The Iraqi Jew smoked on the Sabbath and broke all commandments because they made some sense in Jewish Iraq, but not in European Israel. The God of the State of Israel was nationalism and his Iraqi God was religion.

He had many talks with her. He found her to be aggressive, but sharp and smart. She was beautiful, but she could kill with her look. Her body was warm like a sexy statue, bringing men to surrender to her because of her divine bodily assets. He wanted her to spank him during the game of nudity and nakedness. He was tied with ropes and he paid extra to be humiliated by her. She used a lasso to redden his behind and he became aroused before she placed his banana in her tomato. It was messy and he paid her well. He even had many meaningful conversations with her. They spoke about how she feels and does not feel orgasm. She categorized her clients into addicted, wanting someone else's flesh beside their partners, and young men who wish to relieve themselves because in a society of many virgins, one can find many whores, she proclaimed once.

CHAPTER IV

The Iraqi

The Iraqi kept coming and Habiba kept giving him his animal male requests. There was something very unique about him. He was sometimes brutal in his sexual escapades, but sometimes he was so gentle, like the femininity of a woman. He also always complained that most European women are really men in disguise: their voice, their clothes, and their aggressive demeanor, the way they smoke their cigarettes, their tight pants, and often the disappearance of a manicure and pedicure from their bodies.

"Men are scared of them," he used to laugh with his roaring voice. "They are an unusual distortion of nature." In Habiba he found, according to the pillow talks with her, gentleness and smartness. She combines the two easily and she always accentuates his secure manhood even more. Habiba was a good listener, and through the mystery of chemical attraction of bodies and brains, she began to develop feelings for him. He was spontaneous, direct, obnoxious, and a pain in the behind, but he sincerely believed in his opinions and views of the world. About Ashkenazic Israel, he was terse, short, to the point.

"Ashkenazic Israel," he said often, "took from Arab Jews their Arab dignity and their manhood, and she turned around and blamed them for the difficulties." He even told her that her oldest profession needs to be explained within the racist attitude towards Arab-Jews, and the need for people in her background to economically survive in a society whose God is mainly wrapped up with empty socialist slogans.

Habiba was too involved with her marketing sex and her unique sex with the Iraqi to pay great attention to his periodic ranting. She did things to swallow his seeds because she could see his incredible satisfaction when he shut his eyes and shouted, "Allah! Allah! Allah!" The money began to follow steadily, but she became more selective about her clients.

Passed were the days in which men came to stand in line in the darkness of the transitional camp. Passed were the nights in which condoms were scattered near her shabby tent after their usage. Now she chose the Iraqi. He was older than her, but he began to develop some feelings for her. Her father, the religious Sephardic Jew, had died believing that Israel needed to be like a Jewish Moroccan: religious and naïve. His heart was not able to absorb all the onslaught of Zionist secularism in which religious Arab-Jews were considered some kind of primitive creatures that needed to be reeducated in the promising socialist world. In addition, she did not mind to replace the vanishing father figure with a new one. The new one, the Iraqi one, was offering good shekels, fine clothes, and a humble apartment for her daughter and mother. Anything is better than the old tent dancing in the wind and rain. The stench of humanity in the crowded camps was unbearable, and the very tiny apartment was like a star in her dark sky.

Her periods came and went, but one day in the process of excitement and the game the Iraqi intentionally or unintentionally plowed her flesh field with his seeds. Her body began to look like a huge, inflated balloon. She was bearing an Iraqi-Moroccan child now. In Jewish Morocco, this act could end with excommunication, but here in the land of anarchy, chaos and wars anything goes. Many years ago she had lost the feelings of shame and regret. She was now free to do whatever she wished to do. No communal pressure anymore. In European Israel, pretty and traditional Moroccan Jewish women could become teachers or prostitutes and no one cares. You could even have the right to destroy yourself anyway you wished. Free will is a wonderful thing, she contemplated. The Iraqi even convinced her to swallow some colorful pills, which made her high in spirit. Sometimes they sniffed white powder and she felt like she was in heaven for awhile. Her child being cooked in her tummy had also sucked the stuff, but she needed it more than ever. She noticed that after each act with this substance left her crying in an uncontrollable fashion with her falling into a depression, but her body was longing again and again for these injections. She claimed they gave her feelings of angelic wings. Some pregnant women craved for certain foods, but Habiba craved for her Iraqi and his pills and white powder. She felt this new metamorphosis in her brain, and often she thought that she did not recognize Habiba anymore. She was meeting another persona. The government spoke about redemption of Moroccan Jews in Israel, and she was thinking about her salvation from the secular Zionist slogans around her. After all, most whores in those days were girls, and now they are in the service industry for men who need relief from whatever or just to have fun.

He wanted to inject his seeds into her womb. He wanted and she did not want a creature similar to him. Hesitant and excited, love may conquer anything, but the sexual drive may conquer love. Most men, he thought, need a good, quick sexual encounter, and then they leave emotional attachment to women. Well! It is too late! Her cheeks look like beautiful dates, brownish and sweet. He surrendered again to her eyes, which were like flashlights in a dark room. Penetrating, they expressed desire and longing, either for real love or another dose of the white powder. She is now like a well-oiled machine: compulsive and speedy, self-propelled, predictable, and under this mechanical composition lived a religious Moroccan woman, who became a lady of the night, who was impregnated by two men, who was caught in the web of secular Zionism, who . . . who . . . who . . . .

CHAPTER V

A New Child

Another pregnancy and another sleepless night of heavy breathing and discharged liquids. She wanted to please the Iraqi, and he felt that despite his few marriages, he loved to play the father figure to Habiba. Despite the poison in her veins and despite his illusions on weekends, he would not admit that he had developed feelings for her. Men tend to have late reactions to feelings, and fast reactions to sexual satisfaction. Well, he began to enjoy her face during her pregnancy. The news in Israel was also very bad or worse. Young people were being buried, the victims of Molech war. The army also retaliates against new enemies and infiltrators. The same headlines about death, blood, and sacrifice continued to be the same from the birth of this problematic Jewish state. The left does not know the answer to violence, and the right always came with slogans about preventing violence.

The Iraqi always shrugged it off. He was the one who knew about Arabs, but he was the Arab-Jew who is ignored by Zionist European Jewish Israel. Habiba usually agreed with him, but she was giving him mouth to mouth satisfaction, placing her private parts on his huge opening lips. Her mother left Jewish Morocco suddenly and abruptly with Arab-Jewish history at her heels. She left this world in European Israel without leaving any effect on those who were supposed to absorb her into their secular state. She died believing in angels, holy graves, and sole control of fearful Allah. She believed in the power of the Hebrew and Arabic texts of her prayers. All these turned out to be nonsense. Somehow this rich Arab culture of a thousand years had supplied material for comedians in Israel.

Habiba was just an anonymous number in the human volcano called European Israel. Her concern was her child's birth. The Iraqi loved Samira and now he began to love Amina. He insisted on choosing an Arabic name. The bone cannot separate itself from the flesh.

"We are Arabs," he used to murmur. She did not care about the stares of men who could not help themselves because they loved to look at her feminine assets. Political correctness did not exist in those days, and in her profession she always revealed all of her sexual tricks. She was now busy with her two daughters. New marriage was an archaic institution in her human context. Birth outside the marriage was acceptable in her circles. Her small house, which belonged to the Iraqi, was about ten kilometers from the graveyard of her parents. She could visit them now every time she wanted to ask for real answers to real dilemmas. She was convinced that they could hear her. She cried over their graves with a dramatic Arab emotional fervor. She always felt comfortable and peaceful after these visits. She nursed her daughter publicly, revealing her extended breast and nipple.

She never asked the Iraqi about his occupation. There were rumors that he was involved in a branch of the Sephardic mafia. The Iraqi used to laugh about these accusations leaving her puzzled and confused. However, Allah and the Iraqi were sustaining her well, and no one needed to ask their intentions regardless of their actual activities. He always left early and came home late at night, always hugging and kissing her two daughters. Showering them with gifts was one of his normal habits. She never refused his advances, and without any exception he used to praise his satisfaction of her sexual moves in the dark nights. From time to time he told her some fragmented information about Jewish Iraq, but he never dwelt on details.

She did not roam the dark allies anymore. Now, she accepted only selected clients in her house when the girls were in school. Many European Jews from the ruling establishment came to relieve themselves in and with her body. Life in a tent city was a thing of the past. Morocco was only a memory and her relatives were scattered all over the Jewish state. Her agenda was now her girls, her Iraqi, her clean house, and her income. She lived in her state of mind. The State of Israel was only an abstract theme in which others lived, died, and discussed matters.

For the first time in her life she heard about therapy and she was curious. In European Israel it cost money to ask people to listen to you for the entire hour. The rabbi in Morocco never charged anything. He usually listened to those in trouble and Allah was the formula. The believers swallowed the medicine and tried their best to work with his religious articulations based on faith and devotion to the mystery. The woman therapist was a nice Ashkenazic woman with a great sympathy towards the consequences of the collapse of the Moroccan Jewish tower. She obviously charged Lolita by the hour, but the Iraqi never asked details about Habiba's expenses. She tried to explain that Habiba is reacting to the death of a culture. She tried to convince this incredibly sexy Jewish-Berber-Arab that prostitution is not an immoral act, but it is only a way of survival. Habiba was not sure about the lingo of the chemicals, but she enjoyed talking to a stranger.

The Iraqi just talked sporadically about his hard work and racism in Israel, but his concern was about her and her daughters. The Iraqi thought that the obsession of Europeans with the soul is unhealthy. He was convinced that anyone can help himself if he wants to help himself. Psychology is for those who love to speculate and assume, not for those who seek real help. He often said to her in their pillow talks that if it helps her, then why not, but she should not look for the well of salvation. He believed in faith, logic, and common sense. Man cannot help man. Man cannot help and harm himself. There was nothing less and nothing more. The convictions of the Iraqi were absolute.

The Iraqi was assassinated during his secretive work. The police asked thousands of questions, but she was unaware of the entire context. He was a good man. She repeated her statements. He was a fine provider. The children loved him. The will and the house, the house that he left her, were a total surprise to her. She was in black reading Kaddish in his memory, but he was only a real shadow in her real life. She added a new grave to her visits. The cosmic silence could be careless, she realized in absolute terms. She found some shekels in his personal box in the living room. In his safety deposit box they found a revolver, small bags of heroin, plenty of dinars, and old and yellow photographs of his family in Iraq beaming before the camera with a mosque in the background. The will also left some shekels to his children, the biological and the adopted. He was married twice to Ashkenazic women and, surprisingly, they also found pictures of the graves of the prophets Ezekiel, Nahum, Mordecai, Ezra, and Esther. That was about it. Finally, she realized that his full name was Fathi Dangrun, a famous descendent of a past chief rabbi of Iraq.

Samira and Amina only looked at the coffin, not able to comprehend the sobbing women in the audience. They wore black like their mother and they constantly wished to go the bathroom during the memorial service. The papers described his sitting in the coffee house with his Moroccan friends when suddenly a bomb ripped apart his body into pieces. They stated that gangs of Sephardic Jews were fighting over control of prostitutes and drugs. No one blinked among the readers. After all, belonging to various Sephardic mafias was the only concrete way to build financial and political power outside the democratic processes of European Israel. It is not unusual. More assassinations like this type occurred before. If they kill each other it was not of interest to the larger public. After all, whores and mafia members are only of the peels of onions, which can cause people to cry awhile, but they can also be chopped into their salads.

Lolita-Habiba was the cat with nine lives, who was looking for roofs to experience her survival instincts. In those days the French, British and Israelis had attacked the Egyptians in Sinai in 1956 and hundreds of Israeli soldiers were killed. Habiba knew that Ben-Gurion had made a speech about the wicked Nasser, but she was not sure about the meaning of all the commotion. Her daughters began their education in a relatively decent private school, since Habiba never gave up her obligation to offer them a chance in the moon landscape of the besieged land. Her daughters were introduced to "Uncle David" and "Uncle Solomon" and many other uncles who were not related to Habiba by blood, but by adherence to their mother's flesh. She never heard about Catch 22.

She was already thirty and more beautiful and tired than ever. Tragedies had visited her, but she continued her service to unending lists of men who are looking for a scent of a woman outside their existing spouses and partners. In Tafa the Muslim crier was calling the worshipers to prayer, and Habiba found in the lyrics and melodies this monotonous expression, a feeling of real mysterious belonging to the familiar. Her Hebrew improved and her awareness of people similar to her ethnic background sharpened. She began to see Israel the way it was: many slogans about unity and thousands of tarfs unrelated to Moroccan Jews in their defensive mode.

CONCLUSION

Samira and Amina joined the Israeli army with names like Tikva and Hanna. Habiba was in her late forties, projecting desire to live and love. Her daughters went away from Morocco pursuing the Zionist mythologies of Israeli nationalism. The clients stopped visiting their new humble apartment. She was busy now running a cleaning agency for offices and homes. Most cleaning ladies were young Moroccan women looking for any income for their large families. Habiba knew how to bargain about her financial share in the deals with the establishment and the Moroccan ladies. She was fair, but tough in this financial enterprise.

In her new neighborhood no one knew about her past and no one was interested in her future. She was left alone, making phone calls to army posts and demanding answers about the safety of her daughters. Asking and demanding sexual favors from females were not unusual. Promotions were offered to those who were ready to attach their legs to each other. In those days, high ranking officers in the Israeli army were considered second to the Zionist God. Sexual harassment was an alien concept. Sex was a commodity which was sought by officers in power. Many young women were silent about their disadvantages before the admired macho Israeli officers, who were admired for their war skills. Her daughters were Israeli girls with Moroccan history left sealed in a European box. The keys to the box were thrown far away from this container looking for new locks.

Habiba came and left. No one knew about her birth, her journey, and her departure. Muslim Morocco left her an outsider because she was Jewish. European Israel both ignored her and tried to create a Polish-Russian Jew out of her. Her body served her well, but demanded its toll. Her Allah died a quick death like Moses in legends. Her Moroccan husband saw her as a tactical device for his strategies. Her Iraqi was half human and half savage. Her daughters made it in European Israel: they served in an army which cannot rest because it constantly needs recruits. Samira and Amina both run with Arab blood, but they forget its flow. They tried to be beautiful crows while they were attractive doves in nature.

Everyone celebrated the living. The dead called Habiba was only a legend and a myth. Thank God for writers, who perpetuate her actuality into posterity. Maybe, just maybe, Allah does exist. In only one century from now historians will revise their views about this Lolita. She can be found in all Arab-Jews who know the naked truth about their life and death in European Israel.

RECAPTURING MY IRAQI PAST: JUDEO-ARABIC MYTHOLOGY RESTORED

DR. DAVID RABEEYA

ACKNOWLEDGEMENT

I wish again to thank Mr. Hong H. Ching for his valuable assistance. His typing and editorial skills are appreciated by the author. I also wish to thank again Ms. Arlene Shenkus for her continuous support through years of struggles and victories. Her inspiration and dedication in the past and present times have always encouraged me to express in words my thoughts and ideas through many years of writing about my Judeo-Arabic culture.

INTRODUCTION

One can assume that most uprooted people will adjust to new conditions in their new time and space after years of challenges and difficulties. However, one cannot experience and feel the pain and the despair in this psychological earthquake. As an Arab-Jew who believed in many mythological and legendary aspects of Jewish history in his formative years, I found it necessary to share the implications involved in my settlement in European Israel with other hundreds of thousands of Jews with my Arab cultural background. It is my hope that Arab-Jews who lost their rich Judeo-Arabic tradition will find comfort in the slow and unavoidable metamorphosis in Israel from an isolated European cultural to an inclusive Levantine heritage.

INTRODUCTION

Researchers of many academic disciplines have written extensively on the socio-economic and psychological effects upon those who are abruptly uprooted from their birth place. Often there is a need to distinguish between the status and reaction of immigrants who voluntarily decided to leave their native lands verses those who were forced to depart due to circumstances outside of their personal control.

Many people who leave their country at will may migrate to a new place for economic and financial opportunity and may face problems related to new cultural, religious, social and gastronomic realities, but their own choice can somehow facilitate their acclamation in the environment. However, even in this human scenario, one cannot escape the nostalgic views of his/her past homeland. Dangers may be lurking in the exaggerated memories of former lands, but it is impossible for the human being to avoid comparison with his/her birth place. On one hand, the seed which was formed and nourished in one soil cannot be expected to be removed and planted in strange earth without any modification or difficulties.

Those who experienced any forced movement which has removed them from their natural environment can easily find the common universal elements in the spiritual disaster which befell people whose destiny was shaped by the cruel human waves in the ocean of the racial, religious, ethnic and cultural affinities and one can easily disappear in this human drama of despair, but in this work, the intention is not to discuss the flight of refugees in political terms, but to teach about the human toll which is always associated with their intellectual and emotional deprivation. These oppressive effects on the mind of many can sometimes be perpetrated to include the second and third generations of those uprooted men, women, and children. Furthermore, their conception of the world and humanity can often be shaped by the traumatic and nightmarish scenarios which were witnessed either in their childhood or in their adult life. Mistrust, fear, depression, anger and deep pessimism are not uncommon among these people. Obviously, age is a factor in the measurement and the quality of the new life of the new immigrants. It is generally expected that young boys and girls can, in many ways, make a faster adjustment to their non-native lands. Furthermore, different adults possess various levels of reconciliation with their new, intimidating surroundings. Learning a new language seems to be one of the most serious obstacles in the way to acculturation and assimilation into the new world, in addition to the myriad value judgment decisions facing them on the horizon.

On the other hand, the uprooted may resort to extreme measures to express his/her anger, dissatisfaction and bitterness with the human earthquake which occurred under his/her feet. Accusations are often cast in the direction of those who forced him/her into exile because of religious, ethnic and cultural differences with the majority of his/her native land. The emotional reactions can range from revenge against real and perceived oppression, demands for an apology from those who conceal his/her human tragedy and even deafening silence due to unbelievable frustration and psychological weakness rendering one unable to resist the radical changes before his/her own eyes.

In other words, the concept of earth is being slowly replaced by the concept of a nostalgic, heavenly world. Following the fatherly timely spirit in the new reality frequently takes the place of the motherly soil. Moreover, the disintegration of the communal structure in the process of transition to a new location can urge the uprooted individual to find both replacement and compensation to his/her doomed fate. In this vein, reconstructing, rebuilding and initiating new mythology can become priority in the art of survival.

It is not unknown that the uprooted consciously or unconsciously completely places the mythological and the legendary past in front of his/her financial and economic loss. After all, rituals, prayers, blessings, songs, melodies, idiomatic expressions and life cycle events remain ingrained in his/her mind despite the removal of the territorial space which, to a large extent, is being replaced now by a new dimension called "time".

Within this psychological framework, it is the intention of this publication to both describe and analyze the powerful human earthquake that fell upon Arab-Jews after their departure from Arab and Muslim lands and their settlement in European Israel. The loss of their Judeo-Arabic rich, fast heritage and attempts to reclaim some of its aspects in modern Israel will be the focus of these writings. The rational and irrational dimensions of this incredible human exercise will be explored.

In light of the personal experience of the writer as well as his research of academic theses related to this subject, it is the hope of this writer that this publication will have not only an effect on the uprooted in this world but also shed light on the effects of these water shed events which affect humanity at large even today. It is also possible that those who have utilized the power of discrimination, racism and forced exiles on others may find an opportunity to reflect upon the human devastation caused by their deeds.

CHAPTER 1

Believing in a personal God called "Allah" or "Elohim" can offer some comfort to people of faith. Many Arab-Jews accepted the form and content of this idea taking it to heart, often projecting the patricidal social hierarchy of their Arab and Muslim environment. The Torah came to be the revealed divine texts in which the same personal God took upon himself to personally deliver it on Mount Sinai. The stories of the Hebrew Bible in general and the Torah in particular were conceived as legitimate historical documents. Attempts to question their authenticity were rejected as the work of infidel Jews whose critical perspectives can both endanger and harm the social agreement of the religious Jewish community. "Allah/ Elohim" was the power beyond every particle of nature and reality as well as behind the general events and abstract notions. His name was mentioned tens of times everyday. It is without exception articulated with awe, fear, reverence and hope. His presence and conceived influence never escaped the conversational and the literary religious texts. His omnipresent nature has ruled the mind and the soul of the majority of Arab-Jews. He was the permanent resident in the psyche of children and adults. Almost without exception Arab-Jews prayed to him from their prayer books with sincere innocence and high expectation for rewards in the departments of moral and ethical behavior. He was a terrific and wonderful outsider who can watch every act and perceive every thought. He was in charge in the process and failures of man, ready to severely punish those who intimidate, disobey and question his existence. "Inshallah" (God willing) was attached to every future human plan and offering as well as projected behavior and expectation. He was the king of kings in the everyday life of Arab-Jews. He was feared and loved at once, admired and respected at the same moment. He was the God of the biblical miracles, the God who was the partner of the Jewish people who piloted their ship of destiny through the high and dangerous waves of history.

This God was quite impressed with the performance of Mitzvot (commandments), especially with those which regulate the communal behavior on the basis of the Decalogue. God was supposed, in those past days, to bring the Messiah and restore the Davidic dynasty in Jerusalem. The remote future journey of Arab-Jews was supposed to occur on the basis of Abraham's journey to the "Promised Land" as well as the lofty description of the prophetic texts. Some actually believed that they will fly on the wings of eagles as well as the sudden eschatological war between God and Magog, which will bring an end to the Mesopotamian exile. God of the Torah, with his visions and miraculous performances, together with the dreams and the projection of all prophets as well as the mysteries of salvation and redemption of the Jewish people and the world, was not allowed to be challenged by secular and critical tools. As far as Arab-Jews were concerned the Bible was the text of "was", "is", and "will be". "Allah", "Elohim" has already answered all three universal questions. The world was born by the will of an absolute creator. The purpose of our present life on earth is to perform his commandment and the existence of reward and punishment in the hereafter is taken for granted.

The God of Arab-Jews, not unlike their Muslim counterparts, was praised in songs hymned during holidays, festivals and religious processions. Arab-Jews praised him in Hebrew and Arabic interchangeably with eloquent literacy and linguistic terms. Superlatives were scattered on many social and religious occasions in order to distinguish Him from any other thing. Emotional expressions concerning His love and care of His people were quite prevalent to enable Arab-Jews of faith for a while to put aside their personal agonies and tragedies finding comfort in the greatest of all: Allah!

This Allah was neither a psychological process nor a human idea, thought or concept. God was absolutely and totally separated from humanity. In short, the mythology of God was both the tactic and the struggle of Arab-Jews in their perception of the Almighty omnipresent entity. Losing Allah in European Israel was a devastating and traumatic experience for the majority of Arab-Jews. Existentialism, secularism and socialism were outside their cultural and religious history and many could not bring themselves to recuperate from the death of their "Father in heaven" who was in many ways the patriarch or the sheik of the clannish structure. Feelings of betrayal, disappointment and astonishment were only among the few symptoms of this awful human mourning. Cynicism and fear have often replaced confidence, security and trust with regard to faith and religious commitment. Indeed, the social secular European Zionist engineering of Arab-Jews' life has shocked the human base of the Arab-Jew believer in modern Israel. It is not the purpose of this thesis to discuss the reasons and the motivations of the Ashkenazi secular elite. However, this study concerns the results of the European indoctrinization which had affected the latter in a negative, immeasurable fashion. Suddenly the subjective, nominal, mysterious Allah has become the predicate and the object of humanity. His existence has been dissected by academic sources in the academic discipline called "Criticism of the Bible". Allah was not in the possession of biblical courses in the Hebrew University of Jerusalem. He, without doubt, found his invisible way in the Holy Ark and the synagogue demanding decorum, respect and reverence. Uttering his name was a privilege in the mouth of many Arab-Jews. The word was usually pronounced often with emphatic and intensive quality and those who heard His name have become witnesses to the sincerity of the speaker. They pronounced it at the time of awakening from sleep and invoked it tens of times a day. Inshallah (God willing) was heard at times of difficulties and challenges. Losing this fatherly figure and patriarchal entity left behind many spiritual orphans among many people in the Judeo-Arabic societies.

Allah/Elohim could not have any substitute for a long time to come. Finally, the process of mourning over this irreplaceable spirit may last for the entire life of many Jews born in the Arab lands.

TORAH

Like Allah/Elohim, the Torah was at least holy like the divine. They believed that the Torah had actually descended from heaven. Allah wrote it in all its details, including the vowels and punctuation marks. Many did not know and did not care about the critical modern analysis of the texts. They loved the Torah like a merciful, loving mother who cares deeply about her sons and daughters. Kissing her and hugging her was usually able to send shivers in the bones of those who held her tight to their chest. In their mind, splendor and light were contained inside its letters. She was holy, mysterious, incredible and full of divine beauty. Arab-Jews were accustomed to place it in a splendid decorated silver container with a ringing crown on its top. Opening the Holy Ark with their numerous Torah scrolls has always brought profound happiness; a scene that has reminded them of the glory of the past tabernacle and the temple in the desert and Jerusalem, respectably. Treating this precious book as a secular creation with many human layers was just another traumatic experience in their adopted land, Israel. The dissection of this heavenly scroll into historical periods and various theological schools of thought of ancient Israel were again outside the religious and the psychological framework of the majority of Arab-Jews.

The idea that archeology can prove or disprove the factual items in Allah's book has tormented those who, with all their hearts, believed in the divinity of the Five Books of Moses. The Torah was read and studied and its expressions and idioms were often included in many Judeo-Arabic dialects. Many verses in this same Torah have been involved in and been quoted in many human situations finding in them both comfort and wisdom. Like their Muslim counterparts who adored the Holy Qur'an, these Jews have admired their Torah and drawn from it their solid faith in the existence of a God who will reward the righteous and punish the evil of the world.

Furthermore, this special book was able to protect the people from demonic forces and pagan elements. The inclusion, in addition to its verses, of amulets and charms was supposed to shield the person from personal harm and damage due to the magical insight of its letters. Most Arab-Jews were able to somehow combine their intellectualism together with their rational thinking from a deep faith in a supreme God. This capacity has touched not only the common people but also the religious and the financial and the political elite of their societies. It seems that their scientific explanations of the existence of their surroundings were able to dwell peacefully with their religious beliefs without any major contradiction between these two premises.

BOYS AND GIRLS

In traditional Arab society, gender has determined the directions and the results of one's life. The birth of a girl was accepted reluctantly and, in some cases, emotionally, reflected by the cultural Arab environment of Arab-Jews with worries ranging from her dowry, which was often on the financial agenda, to her future mother and father in-law. Parents often preferred a male heir on the basis of the male oriented system, due to the society's concept of manhood and strength. Females were perceived to be creatures that were frequently irrational in their analysis of human challenges and crises. The domestic domain can belong to them, while men are expected to earn their living outside their residence. Women are expected to be the soft, gentle, feminine human being ready to satisfy men's needs in the biblical knowledge of Adam and Eve.

Indeed, it seems that the cultural consensus by men was that women are not fit to serve as religious leaders of the Jewish community. Her supposed impurity as women, which was well stated in Muslim and Jewish texts, could not prepare her for any serious leadership which requires spiritual or divine blessing. While one can place these perceived attitudes and concepts of women in the realm of mythology, prejudice and superstition, no one can deny the effect of these matters on men's/women's relations in Judeo-Arabic societies. In Israel, the pyramid had turned upside down.

Bringing children to the world was considered the principle destiny of young girls and motherhood is the major purpose of their existence on earth. Mythological and legendary stories and songs about the trickery, character and unreliable trust in women were well known to many Arab-Jews. Men took time to praise women as mother and sister, but many of them have also conveyed messages of warning and fear with regard to the supposed unstable emotional state of the female person. Men and women are expected to be equal. The biological factor was not changed, but the game now has serious legalistic perspectives which forever change the pyramid into a cylinder.

BIRTH

Birth was a psychological or biological phenomenon, but was also viewed as a religious, mystical event which cannot be solely explained in scientific terms. There is a need to protect the newborn and the mother by various tools and tricks in order to avoid the dangers of demons and evil forces. For many Arab-Jews, superstition was an essential element in their human rationalization of the life cycle. The basic idea in their belief is not to extensively talk about the birth of the new child in order to not invite any existing negative forces determined to harm the baby.

The midwife used to utter words in Hebrew and Arabic associated with faith and devotion to her Allah during and after birth, "ismalla eleik /eleiki" (May the name of Allah hover over you). These words were verbalized again and again emphasizing their total dedication to Allah, the protector of babies and mothers, in these critical hours when life and death are in balance. The shrieks during the deliverance of the baby, together with these non-stop religious articulations, were supposed to bring a peaceful result to this tense process of birth.

The transition to Israel where babies were delivered in the hospital has basically removed almost all miseries related to birth. Now birth is treated basically as a biological phenomenon detached from religious and folkloristic expressions. These radical changes in attitudes and expectations have frequently left both disappointment and sadness in the life of many women and men in the Judeo-Arabic milieu. Constructive noise and commotion were replaced by the quickness of the clinical approach. Passed were the special songs and the melodies at the birth of a male child during the ceremony of circumcision.

The ululation of women on this occasion was supposedly designed to chase away the evil eye and all other demons in the room. The throne of Elijah with myrtle was on their mind because it was another way to defend the male child. Occasional spitting on the floor to destroy the evil forces at the arrival of the baby was frequently done instinctively. Eating almonds was supposed to add health to women who deliver their babies at home. Invoking the names of holy men like Rabbi Shimon Bar Yochay was supposed to assist women during their time of pangs and birth, while singing the words of Abu Shabahot (popular poet) can enhance the parents' future in their child's life. In short, the communal and individual mythological, legendary and superstitious beliefs have composed the basis for many explanations and rationalizations in one process of plantation of human needs and their fruitful results.

BOOK 2
TORAH
CHAPTER 2

Certain naiveté was involved in the perception of many Arab-Jews with regard to Jews outside the Arab/Muslim sphere. Some have even imagined that all Jews possess the same customs and mores like themselves. Others, despite their knowledge of European and American Jewry, have assumed that Jews could not but treat each other only on the basis of equality, love and great dedication. Few have heard about discrimination against Arab-Jews by European Jews in Palestine, but they preferred either to disbelieve it or ignore it all together. This mythological concept about the total unity of Jews worldwide on the basis of their common faith was largely and painfully crushed on their arrival in Israel. Furthermore, since they were treated as "dhimmi" by the Muslim regimes, they were expecting in their vision to be treated as brothers and sisters in the formative years of Israel's independence. They soon realized that in Muslim lands discrimination against them was based on religious rationalization of the Pru'an, while in Israel many European Jews discriminated against them because of their Arab culture. The mythology about "klal yesrall" (all Jews are included and equal) was quickly replaced by the recognition that laws of history and nature can easily be applied to Jews like they are to non-Jews. Jews in these contexts were not unique in their supposed moral superiority with regard to other Jews. The power of political and economic control has transcended their mythological Jewish vision which was held dear to their heart for long historical times. Indeed, several conclusions were drawn by many Arab-Jews as a result of many challenges which were presented against their mythological concept of Jews and Judaism. Chief among them is the development of skeptical and doubtful sentiment vis-à-vis the uniqueness of Jews in the realm of ethics and morality. Their self-righteous approach to their Judaism in Arab-Muslim lands was often taken as aggressive and cynical attitudes toward the myth of a shared and common ethical heritage of all Jews. A human party than can discriminate against its own members cannot anymore hold the torch of Jewish righteousness.

BOOK 3
MESSIAH

Arab-Jews were quite impressed with the written and the oral tradition of the Jews and their perspective of the Messiah. Since the verses in the Bible and commentaries on them derived according to their views from divine sources, many of them believed that the Messiah is an actual human being who will create peaceful existence in the universe and bring all Jews to the Promised Land.

The folkloristic notion about the humble and the righteous Jew who sits at the gate of the city and who will be redeeming all Jews and miraculously will collect them in Israel, the Promised Land, was believed. High expectations for the actualization and concretization of this vision were engrained in the minds of many. On the wings of eagles to the Promised Land was an imaginative and existing reality in their thoughts and dreams. Their encounter with secular Israel has removed once and for all the innocent belief of Arab-Jews in a personal Messiah. It became clear that the European Zionists were the people who built the foundation of Israel by human force and energy, unrelated to any divine action by their Judeo-Arabic God. In conclusion, losing an idea without finding an alternative could easily wear out any believer.

BOOK 4
THE LAND OF ISRAEL

They took the idiom land full of milk and honey literally. Hundreds of legendary and mythological premises were superimposed on the reality of the Promised Lands by Arab-Jews. Many Arab-Jews unconsciously imposed their vision of a future Israel on the basis of visionary biblical and post-biblical texts. They are convinced that modern Israel will be the land of pious Jewish men and women, not unlike their perception of the behavior of the Patriarchs and Matriarchs. In their dreams the Temple will be found the way it stood during Solomanian times and the priest and the levies will be singing and sacrificing the animals. Kosher food will be served in every institution, every school and every home. Prayers will be conducted constantly and the Jewish kings will be riding their golden chariots. Most of them were uninformed about the secular, socialist Zionist idea which principally rejected Jewish religious laws and customs.

They expected spirituality and kindness to prevail among Jews regardless of their ethnic and religious background. In short, in their fantasy, the Torah was supposed to become the constitution of the idealistic Jewish state. In this visionary state politics is unknown and political control by one group of other groups was unacceptable in their naïve, religious views of those Jews. The collapse of these legendary and mythological concepts in their many encounters with European Israel has forced many Arab-Jews either to partly or totally depart from their religious past or to establish new cultural and religious mythologies in their adopted land, Israel. Nostalgic views about their religious life in their native Arab lands, as well as supreme praises to the geographical landscape of the past, have become important tools of psychological survival in a foreign and hostile environment.

SCHOOLING

Utilizing psychological processes in order to explain the idea and practicality of schooling were the foundation of the educational concepts for many Arab-Jews. For most Jews in Arab/Muslim lands the trust of educational contents has concentrated on the religious and the theological perspectives of Judaism. While students from middle class families have joined secular schools like Alliance Francais, the majority remained loyal to their religious educational institutions. The fact is that even those who attended governmental schools could not exclude the learning of Jewish texts as a supplementing structure to their semi-secular education.

Mastering the Arabic language was essential to the educational, economic and political success in many Arab lands. It was not unusual to find, indeed, distinguished Jewish Arabists in many Arab lands who have excelled in the scholarly and the teaching segment of the academic community. Arabic represented power, control and economic opportunity for Jews who constituted only a small fraction in a large majority population of Muslims. The general perceived ideas about learning of children have usually accepted the premise that children can learn only through strict discipline and uncompromising respect toward adults. Information and knowledge are important but often cannot be disattached from moral and ethical compositions.

The physical punishment of undisciplined children was frequently based on the assumption that children by nature are unsophisticated adults who need to be pushed to adulthood by sometimes inflicting pain on them. In this way they can feel first hand the consequences of their foolish behavior. Allah, the greatest educator of all, is on the top of the hierarchy of the kingdom of discipline and he endows parents with the authority to control their children. In European Israel the Allah of Iraq was pushed aside by the European secular Zionist socialist ideology of Israel, leaving many Arab-Jews without a sturdy religious anchor to tie their mental ship to the walls of the new harbor. Allah, the father in heaven, and the earthly father, who is the head of family, have lost their power and mystery.

They were often replaced by doubts, cynicism and an unbalanced, realistic view of a collapsing world. Indeed, mythological and superstitious beliefs may be outside the realm of the rational, scientific aspect of the natural laws, but losing the former can create a world of dark shadows without the sunshine of their perceived divine. The main purpose of schooling in the mind of many Arab-Jews was to accumulate information and knowledge and not to teach students the art of socialization with others in their future life. Parents were, after all, the major entities in the installment of moral and religious values in the soul of the child endowed with these privileges by Allah, the great.

FRIENDSHIP

In a society in which the sexes are largely separated, it was unusual to develop friendship between men and women outside the constructional legal marriage. However, profound friendship between women and deep friendship between men were not unknown among Arab-Jews. In traditional and close knit Arab societies, this friendship can last for a lifetime and can persuade itself into the life of their descendents for generations to come. In a society which traditionally permitted friendship only after marriage, several outlets were also in the background of the social fabric of the communities.

One important outlet was the engagement in hidden homosexual activities by men and women as well as the need for the service of prostitutes. Prostitution was somehow accepted by most Arabs as a practical device for social stability, despite the religious rules against these practices. After all, the idea was that in a world of many virgins one can expect the existence of ample prostitutes. Masturbation was common as a human instinct to strong sexual urges, but the social code created false, nightmarish scenarios about its effect on those who are involved in this activity.

Sex education was considered a taboo in many segments of the Judeo-Arabic society due to the deep rooted concept of shame with regard to publicly discussing these intimate issues. In addition, the general view was to leave this delicate topic to the responsibility of parents despite the fact that they rarely brought this topic to the surface of any discussion. Friends were sometimes ready to sacrifice themselves to defend their buddies. However, in some Arab societies the emotional closeness to a friend can be vehemently exploited.

TEENAGERS

In traditional Arab society the subject of sex is considered to be taboo as far as teenagers are concerned. The general idea was that intercourse and other sexual activities must be conducted privately and secretly far away from children and teen-agers. Many boys associated masturbation with sin and some even believed the superstitious notion that this activity can lead to blindness. Homosexual activities between brothers and other male friends were not unknown by segments of the Judeo-Arabic societies.

In general, teenagers were not expected to talk with their parents about radical physical changes in their bodies. Misinformation and distortion of the biological and the psychological implications were available to those who were left by themselves to rationalize the inner natural demands of their young bodies. Men and women are encouraged to marry during their young age in order to fulfill God's commandment as well as to satisfy their sexual appetite. In Israel the codes of sexual behavior, family planning and marriages have altered drastically, leaving many Arab-Jews to educate themselves in the secular and confusing codes, disattached from religious laws, customs and mores.

WEDDING

The belief that the jubilation of women can chase away the evil eye was essential in the middle of the nuptial ceremony. The virginity of the bride was associated with the fruit of the body and of the soul and an unavoidable situation needed to grant moral and ethical conduct in marriage. After all, Allah is watching over everything and everyone and, therefore, he demands total devotion to proper behavior, including the retention of virginity before marriage. Presenting the blood after the first intercourse of the bride was done, often showing it to the relatives of the groom in order to prove the righteousness of the new wife. Matchmakers who are honest in their presentation of the qualities of the two sides before the wedding ceremony can receive positive credits in the world to come because of their fine virtues which are appreciated by Allah/Elohim. The bride and the groom are without expectations and are always surrounded by relatives in order to avoid a great anxiety and fear from the unknown on the marriage night. It seems that some mythological ideas and concepts about the joining of male and female was somehow encased in ancient Mesopotamian rituals as well as in the dominant Islamic culture of the Jewish world of eastern Jewry. Together with biblical rabbinic and medieval superstitious beliefs, these were also added to the mix of both in order to enrich the folkloristic heritage of Arab-Jews. In secular European Israel the mysteries of marriages and weddings have faded a great deal due to the introduction of financial and economic competition between men and women. Realistic decisions calculated through pragmatic strategies about children, jobs and housing, to a great extent, replaced the previous Judeo-Arabic social fabric.

MARRIAGE

Accepting the mythological interpretation of Genesis One in which God commanded people to be fruitful and multiply was the basis of any marriage. Children are the blessing of Allah/Elohim and having many children was supposed to demonstrate the incredible manhood of men and the fruitfulness of women in the divine context of consent. One should avoid talking about sexual activity since God, according to many Arab-Jews, wished to keep all intimate relationships in the family box. Excessive talks about sex can invite the evil eye to stray in order to remove or decrease the attraction between the married couple. Married relatives were considered a safe and human harmony transcending the genetic trap in this arrangement. Masturbation can blind the person and dispersing the seed in vain can result in an awful consequence such as incurable illness and even death. Sexual satisfaction of the female was often considered to be an invention of secularists, not traditionalists. In their view, the satisfaction of the male in this area is one of the most secure systems to preserve the integrity of marriages. The sounds of ululatin during the wedding ceremony could remove negative forces at the location, opening the door for a peaceful and harmonious married life. Sexual education was thought to be the work of ungodly people who wished to transfer the authority of Allah and parents to strangers eager to corrupt their children. It is the conviction of many that the feminine aroma from the body of women can only lead to inappropriate immoral conduct before the wedding ceremony. Men need to be in charge of women's sexual behavior, especially before the marriage since the man's own sense of dignity and honor was supposed to be placed on the purity and virginity of the weaker gender. By the same token, barren women are the sole responsible party in the obstacles upon birth and they basically are disposable to the whims of men who often prefer to remove them from their lives. Fear and reverence of women were not outside the Jewish rabbinic tradition as well as the Arabic culture and many Arab-Jews inherit both civilizations in this crossroad. In Israel the collapse of male domination has forced Arab-Jews to reevaluate their mythological and legendary perception of women and their function in the world. They were left between the nostalgic view of the centrality of men and the new reality of Israel in which men and women compete for power and control; while homosexuality has existed in many Arab societies. Many Arab-Jews have preferred to close their eyes and ears since the practice was considered to be a sinful one in the eyes of God and man. The same has applied to lesbians. The idea that a woman can engage sexually with another woman was not needed to be condemned and punished by the community because this act is both offensive and disgusting in the eyes of the entire universe.

THE HEREAFTER

Many Arab-Jews took it upon themselves to believe in the concept of the hereafter. Mixtures of Muslim religious ideas in their surrounding as well as fragmented rabbinic descriptions have brought them to accept the existence of paradise and hell. Many even believed in the moral and religious ideas of reward and punishment. In other words, somehow, somewhere, either in this world or the world to come, evil people will be severely punished and the righteous will be rewarded generously by God. It seems that this conceived mythological notion has sometimes assisted Arab-Jews in their personal difficulties as well as their suffering as a religious group by the hand of radical Islam. Fear of the Day of Judgment was well embedded in the mind of man who believed that good deeds in this physical world will grant good credits in the next world in God's calculation of men's deeds. Sincere intention in prayers and deeds, as well as financial contributions to the needy and the unfortunate, together with honest repentance, can, in their views, accelerate the process of success in the eyes of Allah/Elohim.

Arab-Jews have often poured their heart into their prayers, especially on Rosh Hashana and Yom Kippur, convinced that emotionalism at the time of their supplication can grant them peace and tranquility in their future on earth and in heaven. The belief in a Jewish, personal Messiah who will rescue Jewish individuals and groups from the trials and difficulties in this world was impressive and has kept optimism and hope in their human agenda. Since their God was basically a personal God in their opinion, they sometimes took the prophetic and rabbinic statements and promises about the Messianic days in their literary fashion. In Israel secularism has created doubts and cynicism when applied to the power of prayers in general and to the concept of Messianic salvation in particular.

ART

The mythological stories and legends of the Hebrew Bible were essential sources for the social and the psychological stability of Arab-Jews. Many expositions of the biblical texts were also an integral part of their rationalizations and explanations of their human universe. Plays, sketches and tales were formed and many commentaries from the Jewish oral tradition were incorporated into their discourses and speeches. However, the prohibition in the Decalogue concerning images, pictures and statues of the divine have somehow hindered the creative possibilities in the fields of artistic expressions in pictures and drawings. However, journalistic literacy and linguistic demonstrations were contributed by many Judeo-Arabic artists combining their Jewish religious faith with the influences of the Muslim culture around them. Many of them have also excelled in scientific, economic and financial enterprises since education was the historic guidance of the Jewish people through hundreds of centuries. Poets, philosophers and writers of prose were many and their contribution to the Arab and the Jewish cultures were well appreciated and recognized by friends and foes alike.

Exhibitions of photography by Arab-Jewish artists were common in those days, since the community, as well as individuals, found this medium to be both fascinating and exciting. Furthermore, adding dark and heavy colors to the photographs of the extended family was considered to be an expression of love and care. Ingrained in the Arab culture, Jews often added pictures of flowers, birds and romantic expressions in and around wedding pictures with eloquent and sentimental utterances added. Often the standing and the sitting positions of individuals in pictures represented the patriarchal society of many Arab-Jews. Many Arab-Jews were composers of Arab music and it was not unusual to find popular bands entertaining audiences with their haunting, attractive Arab tunes and tones. The "ood" (Arab guitar), the "fiddle", the drum and the Shepard flute were the major musical instruments which frequently hit minor keys with unpredictable lengths of quarter and semi tones. A man called Abu-shebahot (master of praises) was the town crier who used to complement the bride, the groom and their families at their wedding. Spontaneous and eloquent poetic words of praise were cast in order to increase the happiness of the joyous occasions in the Jewish life cycle.

Some Jewish women called "deqqaqat" (paid mourners) used to sing dirges at the house of the dead, encouraging the mourners to continue their belief in Allah/Elohim. Mixed dancing was not encouraged, since some Arab social codes have preferred to keep the sexes separated until their wedding night. However, with the introduction of English and French cultural customs and mores during the period of colonialism, some Arab-Jews allowed their sons and daughters to dance together with the other sex under the watchful eyes of the adult chaperones. On the other hand, men often danced with men and women danced with women. Belly dancing was accepted as a legitimate artistic and social activity, despite the strict sexual conduct imposed on both sexes. One explanation was that possibly the above entertaining activity may supply an outlet to the suppressed sexual desires. Parents often sang for their children about their love, quoting verses from the Jewish and the Arab cultures. Children were encouraged to sing about their admiration and loyalty to their parents, who offer their life for their security.

THE LOSS OF THE JUDEO-ARABIC LANGUAGES

Losing one's language can often create a cultural and religious void with serious psychological implications. The language represents both the tactical and the strategic human way to establish the process and the result of our visions, hearing and thinking. In short, the native language of an individual is essentially the psychological parents of the speaker. Their demise can easily create an empty orphanage for those who psychologically lost their begetters.

The Judeo-Arabic dialects, the language of many Arab-Jews has basically reached their final expression in Israel with their settlement in this country. Hebrew has become the dominant language, removing almost all traces of any language which had combined Arabic and Hebrew imparted by Jews from Arab lands. The Arabized version of Hebrew words and idioms which had connected the Arab-Jews to their Jewish tradition has gone. The proverbs, the religious and popular songs, the legends, the stories, the jokes, and the religious hymns with their melodies all disappeared in the secular Zionist environment of Israel. The European founders of Israel had either demonstrated indifference to the disappearance of the Judeo-Arabic cultures or had encouraged their disappearance, but they did not contemplate the preservation of languages in which the terms "Arab" or "Arabic" were found. After all, the agenda of the European secular Zionists was to pursue their socialist ideology in which Russian, European Hebrew and Yiddish were the linguistic vehicles to establish and reform the culture of Israel in its formative years. In those days Arabic was considered either the medium of funny curses or a few gastronomic expressions and idiomatic wishes for the demise of the Arab enemy.

CLEANLINESS AND MEDICINE

Many Jews in Arab lands, like many of their Muslim counterparts, considered cleanliness as an important factor rooted in their religious principles and beliefs. The slogan "clean bodies lead to a clean soul" was often declared by both children and adults. It was customary in those societies not to publicly talk about body waste and other bodily functions. It was considered to be a serious offense when a person decided to articulate details of these functions to his family and friends. This set of practices needed to be kept secretive, not like many European cultures in which public talk about the various functions of the body are placed in natural biological terms legitimately discussed in the public arena. Toilet papers were not trusted to take care of business; therefore, a metal container of water had supplied the solution to cleanliness. Deodorant was not fashionable among the majority of the population. In other words, the obsession with the removal of any signs of natural body odor from under the armpits was not known in those days in the Arab East. Soap was the basic tool for the achievement of decent cleanliness of all parts of the human body. Alcohol is officially banned because of the Quranic prohibition in the Qur'an, while Jews and Christians were allowed to utilize wine for their religious rituals. They were naturally aware of the strict public rules concerning drinking alcoholic beverages.

Wine was allowed for medical purposes and vinegar was often used to clean dishes and other utensils. Olive oil was also often used to place it on a slight wound or cut. Crushed garlic was also sometimes put on cuts, believing it can both clean and purify the effected area. Various incense were frequently mixed with warm water in order to both clean the dirty feet and release the pressure from the legs. Red mud with cleansing ingredients was used as shampoo to remove dandruff and to offer shining color to people's hair. Anema was the device used to get rid of irregularity and stomach pain. Sometime some Muslims will not drink with Jews and Christians and some will even break the cup if it was used by the latter. Muslims will eat from Jewish kosher shops, but Jews will not eat from Muslim shops.

The idiom for a fine and exceptional medicine was called dawa-el-Rambam (medicine of Mamonidas) and one of the most constructive fashions to cure the sick according to some Arab-Jews is to insert the fat from the oily tail of a kosher sheep in the meat soup. Doctors who were experts in various medical fields were available and many have used their services either privately or under the auspices of the rabbinic authority, but sometimes Arab-Jews have preferred to use their spiritual and religious leaders in matters related to cleanliness and health. In Israel, Arab-Jews were facing the slow disappearance of the mysteries and the traditional Arab rationalization of time and space. The psychological implications of this sharp transition can be studied in order to find a way to balance the lost past and the difficult present.

PEACE AND WAR

Being a dhimmi (subject to Muslim protection) has to a large extent both defined and determined the status and the fate of Jews in Muslim lands. The social, economic and psychological framework of Arab-Jews among themselves in Muslim society was also dependent on the Muslim sector. In addition, the dependency on the Muslims for physical protection had created a psychological dependency which Jews had accepted. Their defensive mode in the society was enhanced because they lacked the weapons to defend themselves by themselves. The Muslim was conceived as the powerful persona who can utilize his unlimited arms in order to place the Jew in his political inferior place. This religious, historical arrangement was drastically changed with the enlisting of many young Arab-Jews in the Israeli army. The Arab-Jew needed a way to remove his psychological dependency on Muslim Arabs and to meet them in the field of wars and conflicts where the latter have become his enemy in European Israel. An Arab-Jew who was ensconced in the Arab culture needed to fight now against people similar to his own culture. This dilemma which was imposed due to changing historical circumstances has forced many Arab-Jews to quickly remove their fear from the dominant Arab-Muslim and to adjust to the secular Zionist persona in which aggressive military activities were needed to defend the Jewish state. Being culturally an Arab and religiously Jewish had put many Arab-Jews into the context of the psychological "dual loyalty" syndrome. There is a need to explore and research this psychological development. Recognizing that the new secular Zionist European Jews who have sometimes mistrusted the loyalty of Arab-Jews concerning their ideology in Israel especially with regard to their appointments in high security positions, Arab-Jews have often complained about ongoing discrimination against them due to their Arab cultural background.

BAR-MITZVAH

The ceremony of the Bar-Mitzvah has more religious connotation then social connotation. The tefillin and the tallit were purchased in advance, expecting the young adult to wear them for the rest of his life. The concept and the practice of Bat-Mitzvah were not known in the Judeo-Arabic society. The birth of a girl was celebrated in a modest fashion and in family circles several days after her birth but she was not able to go through this transitional ceremony. The Bar-Mitzvah boy was expected to deliver a short lesson in front of the religious community in the synagogue proving his skills in the traditional interpretations of the biblical verses. Sometimes members of the community would ask him to elaborate on certain words or themes in his sermon in order to test his knowledge of his faith as well as his familiarity with the traditional methods of various commentaries. At home a short social ceremony will be held in which food will be consumed, candies will be tossed in the air and blessings over bread and wine will be recited. Facing secular Israel, Arab-Jews were surprised that most secular Israeli parents do not attach any importance to the ceremony of the Bar-Mitzvah. In Israel the issue of economic survival has become the social survival of many Arab-Jews. Many of their sons and daughters needed to leave school in order to sustain their large family. In the process, many religious ceremonies were scarified on the altar of the new dominant secular cultures of most Ashkenazic Jews.

JEWELRY AND OTHER OBJECTS

In many traditional Arab societies women who wear a large number of golden bracelets, rings, ear rings, and necklaces can indicate not only their financial status but also their position vis-à-vis their husbands who bestow upon them these items. These items are expected to stay in the possession of women even in the case of divorce. Silver may replace gold, but it was obvious that this metal is only second in line within the social and the financial ranks of women wearing decorative talismans, charms, amulets, horseshoes and wishbones which were common practice in those days, since the belief concerning evil eyes, demons and satanic forces were well ingrained in the minds of people. Placing the cut hair of a three year old boy under his pillow after the halaga (first hair cut) was followed by many with the conviction that this act will bring blessings to the boy's life.

Bringing parsley to the dedication of a new house is considered to be a fine omen in order to both chase away the evil eye and bring new blessings to the owners. Undisciplined children are temporarily sometimes tied with a string and cards with words of rebuke can be attached to the chest of lazy and mischievous teenagers. In Israel much of this has changed. For example, the status of many women is often determined by their income. Their economic independence has turned upside down the social and financial pyramids of both men and women.

DISCRIMINATION

Many Arab-Jews believed in the messianic views of the ingathering of the exile into Israel. They also accepted uncritically the notion that due to the difficulties of Jews in history they will be united and care for each other in the literal and the philosophical meaning of the words. Their perception of Jewish life was based on their life in Arab and Muslim lands, unaware of the many and radical differences between themselves and European Jewry. Many of them did not realize that beyond the mythological notions of an undivided religious and cultural Jewish world one can find the dynamics of control, politics and intimidation of various Jewish groups. In Israel these Jewish groups were the dominant Ashkenazic European groups ruling over Arab-Jews who were the new comers in the formative years of Israel. While Israel never had a legal discrimination policy anchored in her laws, the reality was that many Arab-Jews were in actuality subject to discriminatory practices by the powerful Ashkenazic establishment as well as by some Ashkenazic individuals. Inferior housing, jobs, educational facilities and medical structures were offered to Arab-Jews in comparison with their counterparts in the communities of European Jewish immigrants. Basically, Ashkenazi political leaders, the people in control, were able to utilize their awesome economic and financial power to both control, direct and manipulate the direction and the results of the absorption of Arab-Jews in Israel.

In the eyes of many Ashkenazi Israelis, Arab-Jews were Arab human beings who supposedly lacked the basic knowledge of modern civilization. Through social engineering processes, the Ashkenzic leadership wished to form Arab-Jews into their secular Eastern European world by denying the latter their natural Arab heritage in cultural and religious terms. Needless to say, disappointment, resentment, anger, frustration and hatred have become an integral part of the human fabric of many Arab-Jews after the collapse of their mythological conception of Jewish unity and fate.

COLOR AND MESSAGES

Color can represent moods, characteristics and cultural symbols. In traditional Arab societies in which Arab-Jews have resided for hundreds of years, they possessed their own interpretation of the rainbow. Green is the color of Israel; therefore, Jews have often adopted this color as the color of purity and correctness. Pictures, towels, papers, handkerchiefs and cloths have frequently selected the green color as their dominant color in addition to blue and yellow. The color blue was believed to chase away the evil eye; while gold and silver can indicate nobility status and honor. Pink is the color of women, considered to be soft and delicate. Brown is the color of native beauty admired in songs and poems, while blonde represents the attractive, specifically in women's hair. Red can sometimes join the yellow to form both hatred and conflict, while white can symbolize purity of the heart. Black is the color of sadness and mourning, while purple can demonstrate bravery and manhood. Obviously combinations of colors can create unlimited numbers of aspects, dimensions and perspectives. It is obvious now that with the introduction of modern technology the messages of colors and their communal and personal area are being developed into additional interpretations and new symbolic ideas are created.

FOOD

Food and intimacy are connected. The small, the fast and the general sensation related to food are an integral part of the cultural milieu of any society. Eating with others impulsively can form temporary closeness which often transcends different ethnicities and religious and cultural bases. Arab-Jews who were culturally integrated in their Arab world have used gastronomic ingredients well known in that cultural universe.

However, Jewish customs have demanded their share. Most Iraqi Jews did not eat meat on Thursdays with various explanations suggested to explain this custom with regard to the reaction to Jews to Muslim and Christian neighbors. On the holiday of Hanukkah the consumption of latkes was not known, but the eating of sweet pasty was well recognized. The blower of the shofar was allowed to drink water several minutes before the conclusion of the fast in the Day of Atonement. In Passover Arab-Jews have eaten date juice called hilleg, which was used in the preparation of the haroset. The matza was often back at home and brown eggs for Passover are a must. Rice, potatoes and bread can frequently make or break a meal, since they are loved by the Arab culture. Yogurt, both sweet and sour, were necessary in any decent breakfast and the meat of lamb was desired by the multitude.

Smoked fishes were considered delicacy in many occasions and popcorn was a snack appreciated by both young and old. Most Arab-Jews have preferred to have pickled cucumbers, tomatoes and eggplants in vinegar with their dinners and suppers, while looking for spicy ingredients in the salads. Salads must include chopped parsley, tomatoes, cucumbers, onions and garlic, with plenty of olive oil and a dash of garlic. In Israel European food was conceived as bland food unfamiliar with the palate of Arab-Jews. The symbols associated with Eastern European food have developed into a serious emotional disagreement between Ashkenazic and Sephardic Jews.

Gifiltefish, for example, had often become the symbol of Ashkenazic cultural superimposition on Arab-Jews, which was resented by the latter. Varieties of meat consumed by Ashkenazic Jews, as well as the manner in which they were cooked, had also created negative feelings among Jews born in Arab countries.

ANIMALS AND SYMBOLS

Animals and their symbols and characteristics are just one of myriad indicators which may determine the uniqueness of a unique culture. The religious perspectives are also often needed in order to pinpoint the particularity of specific ethnic or religious groups. The owl in many folkloristic Arab perspectives is the symbol of trickery and deception. The camel is loyal until the time he easily betrayed his rider.

A delicate woman is like a dove. The horse is noble, free and gentle. The dog is dirty and impure. The hyena can attract the innocent with its haunting sounds because it is cruel and dangerous. The donkey combines stupidity with stubbornness. The chicken is worse than sheep in intelligence and the fish is a stinky creature with dangerous bones. The beautiful voice of the singer is like the sound of the bulbul (nightingale). The lion has a stinky mouth and the cat is unclean and unworthy companion and, like dogs, they must be left in the outside, never to use them as pets. They are the creatures of the wild, not of domestication.

Animals are diligent and spiders are fine detectives. Scorpions are symbols of evil and conspiracy, especially the yellow ones. Snakes are those people who can plan an attack while placing peaceful smiles on their faces. Elephants are smart, but unpredictable. Mice are the most disgusting creature on earth. Monkeys are entertaining, mischievous and funny. Worms are slimy and can describe a "smooth" liar who tries "to get away with murder". Flies are people who are a nuisance and have disturbing characteristics. Bears are lazy, slow and spoiled people who hate to work and lizards are just the lowest of all creatures in the areas of humility and humbleness. They are also like people who glue themselves to other people and do not allow them to breathe.

The turtle is slow, but steady and they are like people who achieve a great deal on the basis of their decisions. They always finish the race due to their resilience and patience. The hare is a cute animal, but it runs to make quick decisions without involving the process of thinking. The Arabic dialects of Muslim Jews and Christians possess thousands of adjectives and proverbs in which the names of various animals can be integrated within the idiomatic formula indicating the many virtues and traits as well as negative characteristics of men and women. These descriptions can only add eloquency to depictions of various and diverse human beings on this planet.

CONCLUSION

After years of frustration and bitterness it becomes necessary to open a new chapter in the annals of the Israeli state. Mythological perspectives about Jews and Israel must be learned, but one cannot sham reality and facts, despite their difficult and painful memories. One cannot articulate the absolute truth without the emotional and intellectual price associated with those who were oppressed. Nevertheless, it is crucial for those who went to hell and back to tell their stories before the clock hits midnight.

FAREWELL, MY PRECIOUS PAST: JEWISH IRAQI EPILOGUE

DR. DAVID RABEEYA

PART I

The loss of one's birthplace can often become a continuous occurrence that can unconsciously accompany the person throughout his entire life. Indeed, being uprooted from Iraq as a teenager has not only affected my perception of the world and its people, but also has influenced the core of my mysterious self. Despite my accumulation of tragic and joyful experiences and the movement to a new land, Israel and America, this continues to play a crucial part in my understanding and rationalizations of the divine, the religious texts, and humankind.

In my continuous and constant dialogues with myself, even after a half-century of separation from Iraq, the Arabic expression "Sharib haleeb ummu" ("The one who drinks his mother's milk") has always surfaced in my intimate thoughts about the country and its people. This expression connotes the idea that a baby who drinks from the bosom of his/her mother will always be loyal to her. The milk, in my mind, was always associated with the waters of the Tigris and the Euphrates, as well as with the fruitful earth with its pitch-black oil.

Baghdad of the fifties was relatively a town with all the sounds and the smells of any Mediterranean city. The muezzin was calling to Muslim believers to attend their prayers. In Baghdad, particularly, the heat and the sweaty summer could not be ignored. Sewage systems were only installed in middle-class and rich neighborhoods. The bawabs were still standing near some buildings directing people to their apartments and absorbing words of the gossips beyond the closed doors. They were hearing similar stories about fights, reconciliations and intrigues in the large extended families of most Arabs.

I can still smell the aroma of the local open market in which flies, people, animals, and food have somehow found some harmony in this noisy and not-so-clean place. Some men were wearing the dishdasha and most women wore the abayas and the fushi to protect them from horny men. Some men wore franji western clothes and some wore the kaffiya and the agal. Coffee houses were also filled with many unshaven men, sipping sweet tea and shouting the numbers of domino pins and well-worn cards. On my way to school I saw many of them sitting, playing, gossiping far from their wives and children, enjoying the company of other men. Abu-sagga was pouring cold water in a copper dish to quench their thirst for money. I was always amazed by the preciseness with which he poured the water directly into the dishes without any spills. My astonishment as a child was that he never used his hands, but he only bent slightly to allow the water to aim from his giant jar, which was placed on his shoulders and attached by black leather belts.

Sweet candies were everywhere: melabass, zangula, baglawa, malfoof, luzima, halqoom, sugary fistaq, halabi and almonds, and varieties of nuts. For children, these exhibitions of such sweets were another miraculous, heavenly manna. Kurds, Arabs (urban and villagers), as well as Bedouins from around Baghdad, were always rushing to sug-el-shorza making deals, bargaining, and competing. They sold everything under the sun of the city: needles, threads, sewing machines, gemar, zaatan, fums, kosher and non-kosher food, fruits, vegetables, various kinds of dates and figs, bamya, pomegranates, parsley, green onions, potatoes, rice, mango slices, sammon, hibiz (I can see roasted dow with its white interior even now), cucumbers and tarousi, eggplants, pita, pepper, and chocolate. The dry foods were imported sometimes from India (i.e. bharat and anda), Syria (i.e. beabel qadrashi), and Turkey (i.e. halqum).

Accompanying my father to the market was a gastronomic adventure and a psychological trip. Often some Americans and Turkish men wearing their own unique clothing were chatting between themselves in languages other than Arabic. Christians, who were more culturally Arabized than Jews, have hidden the cross under their sweaters, shirts, and coats, while Jews were reluctant to wear the Magen David just to avoid troubles with the high-tempered Muslims.

The reality of Baghdad was and is and always will be with me, but the fantasy and the imagination of the child never left me alone. The myriad colors of the fabrics of Persian and Iraqi merchants were always in a display imitating the heavenly rainbow, while the amobe and the bubbly water of the nargila only added an ambiance of an integrated world in which every item was by itself and with others at the same time. Sug-el-sefafeer was particularly noisy. Rows of stores of blacksmiths, silversmiths, and goldsmiths stood in one linear dimension. The sounds of hammers were deafening, indicating the struggle of the professional with their metals. These merchants have always welcomed you with their flowery Arabic expressions, but they were frequently exaggerating their price and sometimes were cheating you while you were searching for a clue. Smooth people in the 'fast lane' could be found in every space of this human fabric.

Where there were men, there were prostitutes, or visa-versa. Men controlled the purity and the morality of all women, but the male gender allowed some of them to break the rules in order to satisfy the libido. In the coffee houses you could smell the hail (cinnamon) and the nana (mint) in coffees and teas. You could also sporadically see the hakawati (the storyteller). He was just one of the congregant sipping his black drink, but he was endowed with imagination and past tradition. Adult males sat quietly sometimes to listen to the agonizing love adventure of Antra wa-Abla and other fantastic heroes from and Arab and Muslim folklore. This is a scene that has repeated itself thousands of times in the last hundreds of years. I sometimes listened intermittently to segments of these incredible tales and stories, which could bring the listener outside his difficult reality. Sometimes the people around the hakawati were laughing, crying and even interrupting the storyteller to change the direction of the story with new plots and intrigues.

When I saw the movie about Anton Wa-Ahla I also wanted to ride on horses, make love to pretty women, and be admired by others. It was a nice, childish dream, but I somehow sanctified these moments in my heart forever. I always envied the mazza served to this audience, which sometimes was found before my meals at home—tinshi, tiny sambusak filled with onions and tomatoes, red and white vinegary pickles, eggplants, and tomatoes. I can still taste them just talking about them.

Sometimes these men would slip a little arag into their stomach to feel funny and joyful, and I vividly remember my father doing the same before the rituals of the Sabbath. I can recall the small greenish bottle released from his coat, which had transferred him into a devoted religious Jew; he followed his heart and sang the Judeo-Arabic poems before our meals.

I could not miss the fact that I am a Jew. I lived with Jews in one small section of the city, where the mosque was about ten blocks from my house. The cycle of life only reinforced my identity as a Jew living in a Muslim country. The Jewish cycle of life was in the interior and exterior of my existence: the prayers, holidays, poems, celebrations, customs, mores were all Jewish colored by my Judeo-Arabic language (sharh). So, too, were the melodies transferred from generations of Iraqi Jews to their descendents. The synagogue was a place in which individual Jews could find support at times of anguish and tragedies by pleading with their personal God. In addition to Elohim, He was often called Allah, because of this dominant utterance in their Muslim environment. The synagogue was also a place of communal gathering, seeking information about Jewish life outside their local Jewish environment. The administration of the chief rabbinate used to send their agents to various synagogues to announce important events in Jewish life. These announcements often included the dates of the opening of Jewish school, the price of kosher food, the call for contributions to the needy, and opportunities for new positions and volunteerism within the Jewish community.

The Jewish community was in existence from time millennium. It built a sophisticated infrastructure of educational and religious institutions and organizations. Many Iraqi Jews know about this phenomenon, while others are not informed. This was not their first interest!

PART II

While one can find most information about Iraqi Jews in many agents of modern communication, it is difficult to understand the loss of this community after it was swept away by history without asking living witnesses to complete the picture, since the last Jew left Iraq after residing in its area for thousands of years. It is not an exaggeration to declare here that the end of the life of this community can constitute a watershed in the history of the world for Jewish people and the Middle East. Roots of individuals and communities are being uprooted absolutely and totally by the waves of power outside their control, while the cosmic silence is always indifferent to human concerns, tragedies, and hope. Nevertheless, it is mandatory that the testimony of those who suffer the loss must be recorded.

Many Iraqi Jews, like other refugees in the troubled Middle East, have lost their human dignity, a matter which can not be measured with money and numbers. It seems that every refugee needs to find his/her way to climb up from the abyss of disorientation and shock, in order to move into a new land with a different sky and horizon. The five senses of the uprooted needed to reluctantly adjust to a new territory in which their ancestors did not reside, and their memories were not anchored in the new surrounding.

Israel of the fifties was this strange and incomprehensible planet to the majority of Iraqi Jews. The sound of Arabic was suspicious to many European Jews. The Iraqi mannerism and gestures, which are naturally accepting in Iraq, have formed a threat to those who never encountered the Arab culture. The code of honorable behavior in Iraq has lost its legitimacy in Israel, because Israel swallowed them in like a vacuum cleaner in the name of unity and security. As a result, a new honorable code was created based on relativism and not an absolute.

The most devastating item is the loss of Allah-God-Adonai Elohim in the process of settling in the new land. He has decided to remain in Iraq, and not to move with Iraqi Jews to Israel. This God of compassion and awe, who cared about His Iraqi Jews, has abandoned them in the land of many atheists and agnostic European Jews. Most Iraqi Jews have also betrayed Him after he figuratively stabbed them in the back. Many of them became cynical towards Him, blaming Him for their plight. In the uprootededness, some even cursed Him because he was a loyal friend who smiled at you, but attacked you in a dark alley. All the emotional melodies to Him and the flowery words in Judeo-Arabic were wiped-out suddenly with a huge school eraser. All the naïve and the innocent beliefs in Him were exchanged with skepticism, doubt, and even mental illness in European Israel. To add insult to injury, they were told by some uninformed European Jews that they are not real Jews. Kafka and Orwell were present in this moment of unbelievable degradations. They, the Iraqi Jews, were there before Islam, and those who never left Iraq can trace in a folkloristic way their roots in the Promised Land.

The European Socialist Zionists together with their religious counterparts had the gall to tell Iraqi Jews about the Jewish identity of Abraham's descendents. God was dead for many Iraqi Jews, and He was replaced by the slogans of Marxism, Communism, and Socialism, which were dear to the heart of the Ashkenazi founder of Israel. So it turned out that the Torah is not a divine text anymore. Another surprise! The heart can endure many surprises, but not this giant one.

All the kissing and the hugging of the Torah were in vain now. All the stories about the past, present, and future events in the Torah are only a legend. It is impossible! There existed some kind of misunderstanding of thought within religious Iraqi Jews (most were religious). They discovered in secular European Israel that the Torah is like any other book written by men. Allah was not involved in its creation, they were told.

The Iraqi Jews were brown and those European Jews were of a different color. Is it possible? In Iraq we assumed that all Jews looked Jewish-Arab. The mind was filled now with contradiction, confusion, despair, hayna laughter and inner explosions of human TNT. The weak in body and spirit just vanished according to Darwinism. The strong continued to survive with the scars of self-bitterness and the lava of anger hidden behind the new standards of proper behavior in the European universe. In those days, even the strong had internalized in their brain the germs of racism and an inferiority complex, as well as thousands of questions of why with zero answers. Are we not Jews? It was just false. They, the Iraqi Jews, were the real Jews. Those Iraqi Jews, who were not largely assimilated in the non-Jewish world, are called now non-Jews, but European Jews, of whom many went beyond acculturation and became totally assimilated, are now judging who are considered authentic Jews from Mesopotamia. Iraq celebrated itself with tragedy. It was not a comedy. It was the hell of heaven descending to earth.

PART III

In Iraq Jews were officially members of the Taifa-el-Yearalim (The Israelite [Jewish] Community). This was placed on various legal documents of identification. We were subject to Muslim protection for many centuries. This arrangement has intermittently lacked political and economic stability of various Ottoman, English, and Iraq Muslim regimes, and they have determined the position of the Jews. Sometimes they were able to thrive and sometimes they were pressed to the wall, unable to gain their basic rights. The British have decided to promote the minorities (Jews and Christians) often at the expense of Muslin Iraqis.

Some Ottoman Sultans somehow opened the economic system for Jews when they became Ottoman subjects, despite the opposition of religious Muslim leaders. Treatment of Jews during the monarchy has depended on the attitude of kings toward their minorities, interior political development, and exterior events by the powers. This up and down syndrome of existence left Iraqi Jews depending on divine power. They were convinced in their heart of hearts, against all national odds, that somehow Allah will close many gates, but He will open many others for them.

Political attacks, massacres, and political oppression could not remove the belief from the majority of Iraqi Jews of the incredible power of God and his capacity to punish and redeem. The hachameem (the rabbis) have preached on Saturday afternoon on the political difficulties of the Jews, using biblical and rabbinic references due to the censorship in the Muslim environment. This argot device had assisted many Jews in their plight. The decoding was obvious to the audience of Jews and the messages were absorbed without any difficulty. Some Muslims called their Jews insulting, degrading names and some were emphasizing the common heritage with the Jews because of Abraham, Ibrahim, the father of us all.

Many Iraqi Jews took all this complexity of attitudes of various Muslim groups and individuals and continued to dream about their fantastic messianic days in which they followed the religious journey of Abraham to the Promised Land. The images of Eretz-Yesrael were explained in their minds on the basis of the religious texts they have studied and cherished. These imaginative views of the Holy Land have convinced some of them, at least, that they find the Holy Temple in Jerusalem after their arrival in that special land. They saw the High Priest, the sacrifices, and the strict enforcement of the Jewish Law (Halacha) as the idealistic future, which will meet them in Israel. They will soon regret the establishment of these unrealistic images when they place their first step in European Socialist Israel of the fifties. Anyhow, the Messiah has not arrived and He will probably take a leave of absence forever, but the people of faith need to experience for themselves the disappointments in order to start to find political power for the sake of any achievement in the economic and financial fields.

Their encounter with secular Israel led them to see people ignoring the laws of the Sabbath, Kosher food, and the customs of sexual encounters, friendships, man-woman relationships, and attitudes toward children. They quickly realized that secular Israel is interested only in transforming them into Israeli nationalists in the European image and making them subjects to the Eastern European culture, which was considered by the latter as superior to the Judeo-Arabic culture. Social engineering was the only game in town and the guinea pigs were the Arab-Jews in the human laboratory of European leaders.

Only nostalgic memories have remained from their rich Iraqi Jewish heritage. Some were interested to hear about segments of their past within the new generation of Iraqi Jews. Some were happy to leave the Iraqi heritage behind them, convinced that it was the only way to be accepted by the dominant European culture. Few took it upon themselves to delve into academic research of their heritage, publishing articles and essays concerning known and recently unknown documentation. However, most Iraqi Jews who migrated to Israel were busy in their attempts to survive economically in the new land, while their sons and daughters, to a large extent, were being indoctrinated by the Socialist European ideology, leaving behind them the Arab-Jewish heritage of their parents and grandparents. The gap between the adults of Iraqi Jewish immigrants and their descendents widened to allow the Hebrews of the Egyptian Exodus to pass through. Life goes on and grinds the past into the containers of the present.

When the structure of the religious Iraqi Jewish community has fractured and became lost in Israel, every Iraqi Jew was left to swim in the slogans of the secular Zionist ideology, hoping to reach any shore for economic opportunities. My relation with Israel was always problematic because of the maltreatment by the Ashkenazi establishment of Arab-Jews during their migration to Israel in the fifties, as well as by the undesirable practices by many governments towards indigenous Arabs of Palestine. Indeed, Sephardic Jews and Palestinian Arabs were in various levels of the two weak political forces in the definitions of the political and cultural composition of Israel and the occupied territories. In historical terms, a mass exchange of populations took place in the Middle East. Many Palestinians were either driven out or left voluntarily, while the majority of Arab-Jews were forced to leave their native Arab countries, partly as a result of the Israeli-Arab wars of 1948 and 1949 and the rise of Arab nationalism.

In Israel Muslims used different names for Jews. In Israel some European Jews were calling Iraqi Jews name like chach-chach (riff-raff), schwartze (blacky), dirty Arab, primitive Orientals and many other names unacceptable to a weak stomach. Many Jews were like a fish trying to survive in a parched land after a drought in the summer of Arabia. The life in the transitional camp for most Iraqi Jews meant that the synagogue never existed in the tent city of the fifties. There were no communities, only scattered individuals disintegrated culturally deprived of their roots and psychologically deprived and separated from themselves. They saw their shadows and they could not touch them. They saw their inner bones without touching their flesh. They were the silent sphinxes, eroded slowly in the sand of the past glory of the Hebrew colleges and Jewish schools.

The majority of the houses of Iraqi Jews have already turned into ruins or new buildings have replaced them. Almost no one knows anymore about the stories of these houses and their inhabitants; stone, bricks, mud, and metals never uttered a word. The graves turned into dust or a new wide boulevard. The synagogues are history. These institutions only confirm the statement "from dust they come and to dust they return." Today almost all Muslims in Iraq have not met a Jew in their entire life, nor have they heard of them. Some old Hebrew words are still hanging on old walls, trying to testify to a glorious past of religious sounds that reached heaven in their sincerity.